I'M SORRY, GROVER
A ROSH HASHANAH TALE

By Tilda Balsley and Ellen Fischer

Illustrated by Tom Leigh

KAR-BEN
PUBLISHING

To my big brother Walter with thanks. – T.B

Dedicated to my husband for his love and support. – E.L.F.

For Sarah – T.L.

KAR-BEN PUBLISHING
A division of Lerner Publishing Group, Inc.
241 First Avenue North
Minneapolis, MN 55401 USA
1-800-4-Karben

For reading levels and more information,
look up this title at www.lernerbooks.com.

Library of Congress Cataloging-in-Publication Data

Balsley, Tilda.
    I'm sorry, Grover: A Rosh Hashanah tale / by Tilda Balsley and Ellen Fischer ;
    illustrated by Tom Leigh.
        p. cm.
    Summary: Grover In Israel, while Brosh is preparing to celebrate Rosh
    Hashanah, his favorite cap goes missing and he fears Grover or another of his
    friends has taken it.
    ISBN 978–0–7613–7560–9 (lib. bdg. : alk. paper)
    ISBN 978–1–4677–1647–5 (eBook)
    [1. Lost and found possessions—Fiction. 2. Forgiveness—Fiction.
    3. Rosh ha-Shanah—Fiction. 4. Jews—Israel—Fiction. 5. Israel—Fiction.]
    I. Fischer, Ellen, 1947- II. Leigh, Tom, ill. III. Title. IV. Title: I am sorry, Grover
    PZ7.B21385Iai 2013
    [E]—dc23   2012027932

Manufactured in the United States of America
3 – DOC – 9/1/15

Hello everybodeee!

This is your furry friend Grover wishing you a *Shanah Tovah*. That is Hebrew for "Happy New Year." I am here in Israel with my favorite Cookie Monster, and I am going to tell you how my friend Brosh learned to be an even better friend in the New Year.

Brosh was sitting in Shoshana's coffee shop, staring at the ground, when Cookie Monster walked in.

They knocked on Grover's door, but no one answered. "Grover loves blue, you know," said Brosh. "In fact, his fur is the same color as my cap. Maybe he took my cap."

"Where you go next?" Cookie asked.

"I stopped to talk to Avigail. There she is now." Brosh waved for her to cross the
street. "Avigail, have you seen my cap? I think someone took it."

Avigail's eyes got big. "Do you think Avigail would take your cap, Brosh? Avigail and Brosh are friends." Avigail walked away quickly, her feelings hurt.

Moishe Oofnik heard all the commotion. "Do I hear the sweet sound of crying?" he asked, looking around. "And you, Brosh, is this a rotten day for you, too? *Heh*, *heh*."

"Yes, Moishe," Brosh said. "I've lost my woolly cap. Is it in your trash can? I walked by here on the way to the grocery store this morning."

"Nope, no caps in my can," Moishe said. "Well, except for a grubby baseball hat that someone tossed away last spring. It still has bird droppings all over it. I wear it only on special occasions."

Brosh and Cookie Monster turned to go. "Thanks anyway, Moishe."

תפוחים

"Here is grocery store, Brosh. Me heard you say you bought food for Rosh Hashanah?"
Cookie asked. "Oh boy oh boy. All this talk of food making me hungry."

14

דבש   חלה   יות

"Yes," said Brosh, "I guess we could look there. But I don't think it's at the grocery store. If Moishe and Avigail don't have my cap, and it isn't at the Coffee Shop, Grover must have it. He must have taken my cap."

Brosh felt a tap on his shoulder. It was Grover.

"Hello, Brosh," Grover said. "Is this not your cap? You were wearing it this morning. I wondered why you were wearing a woolly cap in this beautiful weather. But it is a highly attractive blue color."

"Gee, Grover," mumbled Brosh. "Where did you find it?"

"I went to the grocery store after you left. Hearing about all that tasty Rosh Hashanah food made me hungry. And there was your adorable little hat in the ice cream freezer, right next to the chocolate," said Grover. "It must have been looking for a place to cool off."

Cookie Monster sighed. "Nice place for cooling off," he said. " Right next to creamy and delicious ice cream."

Brosh had his cap back, but he didn't look happy. He felt bad that Cookie Monster had spent so much time helping him look for his cap. "I'm sorry, Cookie," he said. Then he looked at Grover and felt even worse. He had accused him of taking his cap.

"I'm sorry, Grover," he said. "I should have known better. You're my friend." He held out the cap. "You can have it," he offered. "It matches your fur."

"Oh, no, thank you, really! It is perfect for you," said Grover. "Besides, woolly caps make furry blue monsters very itchy."

"Thank you for being such good friends," said Brosh to Grover and Cookie, as he put on his cap. But something still didn't feel right.

"I've got to find Avigail. I need to tell *her* I'm sorry. Shalom."

He raced down the street, thankful for the High Holidays, thankful for a chance to say "I'm sorry." He knew he'd be a better friend in the new year.

About Rosh Hashanah

Rosh Hashanah, the Jewish New Year, comes in the fall, and begins a ten-day period called the High Holy Days. It is a time for celebration. Families and friends gather for festive meals and wish each other *Shanah Tovah*, a sweet New Year. It is also a serious time. We say we are sorry for bad things we may have done during the past year, and we promise to do better in the new year. At synagogue services, the shofar is sounded to welcome the new year. We pray for a year of happiness and peace.

About the Authors and Illustrator

Tilda Balsley has written many books for Kar-Ben, bringing her stories to life with rhyme, rhythm, and humor. Now that *Sesame Street* characters populate her stories, she says writing has never been more fun. Tilda lives with her husband and their rescue Shih Tzu in Reidsville, North Carolina.

Ellen Fischer, not blue and furry, or as cute and loveable as Grover, was born in St. Louis. Following graduation from Washington University, she taught children with special needs, then ESL (English as a Second Language) at a Jewish Day School. She lives in Greensboro, North Carolina, with her husband. They have three children.

Tom Leigh is a longtime illustrator of *Sesame Street* and Muppet books. He lives on Little Deer Isle off the coast of Maine with his wife, four dogs, and two cats.